Jamie Robins is 80 years of age and had his first book published in 2005. He started his writing career 12 years ago after purchasing his first computer. This was because he was unable to pursue his love of playing golf due to arthritis. Since mastering the computer he has written several children's books, murder mysteries, erotic fiction and humorous stories. His only ambition is to have at least three books published within three years.

A FUNNY THING
HAPPENED ON THE
WAY TO THE COLISEUM

Jamie Robins

A Funny Thing Happened On The Way To The Coliseum

Vanguard Press

VANGUARD PAPERBACK

© Copyright 2006
Jamie Robins

A CIP catalogue record for this title is
available from the British Library

ISBN 1 84386 270 0

*Vanguard Press is an imprint of
Pegasus Elliot MacKenzie Publishers Ltd.*
www.pegasuspublishers.com

First Published in 2006

**Vanguard Press
Sheraton House Castle Park
Cambridge England**

Printed & Bound in Great Britain

Dedication

To my darling wife, Claire,
for her patience, support and encouragement.
Although wheelchair bound, she is my rock.

Chapter 1

The Wrong Destination

It was a Friday evening and nearing the end of the current rugby season as Tom Behrens sat drinking in his local pub with his two mates Dick and Harry. By that time they were all a little worse for drink, Tom suddenly turned to the other two and out of the blue suggested that because they had been dropped from their local rugby team for the following Saturday's game they might as well have a day out visiting the old Dome site. Then take in a show at the Coliseum theatre that had some sort of Greek farce show on, and after that have a few jars together around Soho before returning home.

"Great idea," remarked Dick James the larger of Tom's friends as he idly slid his finger through a pool of spilt beer drawing the shape of a heart on the round table while he eyed up his other pal Harry, awaiting his reply.

Harry Fenton, all twelve stone of solid muscle appeared to think for a while before he answered his friends, then said rather blurredly, "Bloody great idea that Tom, we could mooch around Soho and maybe visit a strip club or something?"

Tom, also bleary-eyed, remarked, "Trust you to think of female strippers mate! Anyway I suggest we all meet tomorrow at around 10 am at my place, if that's ok? And I reckon we should hire a cab for the whole day and share the cost, and if we get a little pissed later on it won't matter about getting home safely, will it!"

Some time later after quite a few more jars of bitter, he and his two mates left their watering hole quite unsteadily and headed for home just after the pub's late night closing time.

The next day soon dawned, and on awakening the three of them found the weather quite hot and sunny, so after telephoning each other they all donned tee shirts and lightweight slacks. Dick and Harry met in the town and then headed for Tom's place to await their Taxi.

Around the appointed hour the taxi arrived so the three of them piled into the back of its cold black and slightly scented interior.

Tom addressed the driver, "Morning mate, lovely day isn't it? How long do you reckon it will take to get us up there?" he said, alluding to the old Millennium Dome site.

The driver turned round in his seat and replied in a slight foreign accent, "From where we are and traffic permitting sir, let's say just under an hour. Oh and by the way you guys no drinking in the back of the cab please."

"Of course we won't driver we're reserving our drinking binge for later on! We thought we ought to arrange a rendezvous point for later on where you can wait for us while we are out enjoying ourselves. How about outside the Lyceum theatre about 11pm tonight will that be ok? And would you on behalf of us three accept this tenner and have a meal on us for the wait and your trouble, oh and by the way what's your name?"

The driver replied, "Yannie sir, I'm Greek you know!" He then started the cab and they moved forward on their journey.

"Greek is he, you don't say, he might be able to explain what the play's all about then," whispered Dick as he surveyed the inside of the cab that resembled a foreign travel bureau; all around the inside there were pictures of Greece advertising holidays at cheap rates.

"Looks like a bloody travel agents in here," quipped Harry. "Tell you what you guys I was thinking to myself last night that we ought to arrange a trip abroad just for ourselves one year. That would give our ever loving a break, and us, what do you two reckon to that idea then?"

"Brilliant," replied Tom staring at the pictures of Greece and the ruins of the Acropolis and imagining himself laying on a beach there and eyeing up the local talent.

Just then their taxi suddenly swerved and the three occupants in the back slid to the floor, as Tom shouted to the driver through the glass partition, "What the bloody hell are you doing Yannie boy, trying to kill us?"

"Sorry mate, it wasn't my fault, some silly cow jumped the lights and I only just missed her. Anyway luckily we're nearly at our destination," he added as he surveyed the sprawling trio in the back of his cab as they began to resettle themselves back in their seats.

He also noticed Harry fiddling with a red strap attached to the roof at the back of the cab as he struggled to sit himself upright, so he immediately screamed out, "For Christ sake don't pull on that cord mate, it apparently does something very special!"

Unfortunately, he was just too late with his warning as Harry pulled his 82 kilos up into a sitting position just by using the red strap as a lever!

Immediately there was a blinding flash inside the cab and in an instant the trio of friends found themselves on a hot dusty road sitting in a rickety horse drawn cart, with Yannie urging the animal on with a whip and a few Greek curses.

The first to speak was Tom with a somewhat trembling voice, "What the bloody hell happened then chaps, and where on earth are we now?"

"In Ancient Greece by the look of things, I did warn

you not to touch that red strap didn't I? Now we could be stuck here for flipping ever," replied a forlorn looking Yannie.

"Ancient Greece you say, you must be ruddy joking or something I reckon we're imagining all this somehow or another after that accident!" replied Dick.

"We didn't have one you burke, I missed the silly cow didn't I," Yannie screamed.

"Now will you two daft sods calm down a minute and let's assess our current situation right?" Tom suggested as Yannie pulled the cart to a standstill by the side of the dusty road, as he carried on his conversation by saying, "As I see it guys we are now in the mire right up to our necks, moreover judging by the present temperature out here, very hot mire at that. Now, do you have any idea how we might return home again Yannie, or are we all really dead or just dreaming?"

"I haven't a clue. All I can say is my old grandfather once said if that red strap was ever pulled, all those inside my old cab could end up out here in Greece, then they would have to **earn their** way back, but I didn't believe the silly old sod, so don't ask me how to get home!"

Harry started to moan as he sat in the hot sunshine, "Earn our way back, that's bloody rich that is, doing what? I'm a Banker and I reckon there isn't a flipping Bank anywhere around here for miles."

"Stop moaning and let's press on and try and find somewhere to stay, and hope whoever they are they take credit cards," Dick volunteered optimistically eyeing his other two colleagues.

Yannie started to laugh hysterically and nearly fell off the cart in the process, "Credit cards, credit cards, now I've heard it all. Don't you realise this is Ancient Greece mate and we aren't dreaming either, so I suggest we head for that old Acropolis place somewhere out ahead and see

14

what transpires when we get there, ok gents?"

Before anyone could answer him he cracked his whip and the horse cantered forward as the cart left a trail of yellow dust in its wake. Meanwhile his three passengers hung on for grim death as the cart bounced over the uneven unmade road towards their chosen destination.

Later that afternoon after they had been travelling for about an hour, suddenly the sun seemed to set below the horizon and darkness quickly befell them.

Yannie started to sing in Greek to hide his nervousness; however in the distance they saw a light before them twinkling in the balmy dark summer evening, their driver gave the horse a sharp prod with his stick to hurry him up towards the welcoming beacon of light.

It wasn't long before they came upon a small village containing about six small mud buildings and a stall from where the light that had guided them shone from its oil burning ornate brass lamp.

The stall had food, including fruit and some clothing for sale, and at the rear stood a wizened old man with white hair. Also around the stall stood at least six men and women dressed in white togas who on seeing the travellers arrive, had suddenly stopped talking as the cart approached out of the gloom. Then as soon as the cart came to a halt the crowd turned and stared at the four travellers in amazement, they all started laughing, and pointing at the quartet. When the old man behind the stall shouted in Greek, "Call the guards, we have strangers in our midst."

Before the four companions could alight from the cart, six burly Roman guards appeared holding swords to the ready and quickly surrounded them. The leading guard who was sporting a golden breastplate shouted, "Stand too and alight, you are all under arrest!"

Yannie shouted back in Greek, "What for?"

The guard gave him a slap on the backside with the

flat of his sword and shouted irately,

"For one thing you have just infringed Nero IIs private lodge area, now get down, before I run you through, you unworthy peasant."

The four companions were on the ground in an instant as Tom thought to himself, that was much quicker than their normal 'rugby scrum down'.

The three companions were quite surprised to realise that they had each clearly understood every word the guard had said, how, they did not know. However, Yannie put his newfound agility down to the proximity of the guards' sword sticking in his rump.

"Take them to the holding place, have them bathe and then clad them accordingly," instructed the guard with the gold breastplate. He added pointing to the group, "and remove those stupid legging things, for tomorrow we shall find out from whence they all came!"

When the frightened comrades arrived at the guardroom, they were immediately stripped naked and herded into the nearby bathhouse. Once inside they found it quite warm, and the water was as hot as they could bear. They quickly jumped into the water naked as one by one the guards prodded their bare bottoms with their swords, and at the same time roared with laughter. Suddenly into the bathhouse came six nubile young women carrying oils and loofers and wearing the flimsiest of clothing and without hesitation entered the water and began bathing the four men, much to their liking.

Tom suddenly cried out to the others, "This certainly beats all our rugby baths boys, don't you think?" Just as one of the young women began to soap his already erect penis, and the biggest guard began laughing at the smallness of Tom's equipment.

Yannie suddenly cried out, "Hey you guys, these birds don't wear any knickers!" while at that very moment his young helper bent over to accept his offering of a typical Greek shagging.

Suddenly the cried the guards in unison, "That's enough."

"Out you get it's time for your food, and I suggest you eat heartily it may well be your last meal on this land!"

The four travellers started to shiver even in the oppressive heat as the women rubbed them down with papyrus leaves. Yannie whispered to his young drying companion, "What did he mean by that remark, maybe our last meal?"

She coyly replied, and quite calmly too "Well strange master it would appear you have transgressed into our leader Nero II's territory, and for strangers the usual penalty for that, is death! But do not worry any because if Nero does decree you die by the sword, your execution should be over very quickly indeed because we now have a new executioner named *Lastrighticus* and he is simply the very best one we have ever had. This is what happens on the day set for executions; he first of all reads 'your last rights,' and I am reliably informed by the soothe sayer that he has perfected his ritual over many years, and it goes like this:

"Prisoner before me, relax," then before you know it your head comes off in one chop of his mighty sword."

Yannie, who was already half erect again, thanks to his handmaidens drying technique, instantly reverted to 'Erecticus Flattus' mode as he heard the young maiden's grim news.

"Did I hear her right?" remarked Tom removing his own roving hand from his helper's bosom.

"You certainly did mate," Yannie replied as the leading guard interrupted their conversation.

"Do not worry overmuch strangers, our leader is in a

generous mood this month of the full moon, so you may well escape with only a flogging. So eat heartily and when you have eaten you may each select a hand maiden to bed with you for the night."

Yannie turned to his three cash paying passengers and remarked, "Tell you what you guys, just imagine all these women being **freebees,** you certainly would have had to pay a lot for it back **there** in London, now wouldn't you?"

The four of them rapidly ate their meal of roast pig washed down with copious amounts of red wine, then retired to their beds accompanied by four buxom girls to enjoy a night of passionate love making.

The next morning they were awakened by the guards at early daylight, they could, however, have slept on as they were still quite tired. Moreover, all of them had their knees skinned and sore because being from the twentieth century they certainly were not used to stone beds, with all but a sheepskin to lie upon.

As they departed their four young grateful sleeping partners bid them farewell while the guards ushered them into an enclosed cart and shackled them together, before urging the ass pulling the cart to move forward. Then as they travelled towards their new destination none of them could at the moment come to terms with not wearing any under garments beneath their newly provided pleated white skirts. They found the dry straw in the cart chaffed their bottoms and private parts as it rumbled forward.

Yannie sat staring at his little willie, wondering if he would ever be able to use it like the three times he had the night before! The rest of the quartet were silent wondering what fate had in store for them as the sun climbed higher in the morning sky, and the heat in the confined space of the cart was becoming unbearable. All of a sudden they came in sight of the town of Athinai and with Harry having studied Greek history he knew that in the twenty-first century it was actually the city of Athens they were approaching.

As their rickety cart and the accompanying guards entered the city gates, it headed down a cobbled roadway towards a large open white building with steps leading up to a marble plateau, whereupon sat a resplendent rotund individual sporting a gold crown of fig leaves upon his balding head.

The cart halted at the steps and the occupants were released. The six guards surrounded them and ushered them up the sixteen steps towards the platform area, and once there they were positioned just six paces from the reclining figure. The senior guard instructed them to stand still and be silent, as he addressed the seated figure thus,

"My mighty Lord Nero II, we have brought before Your Eminence four strangers who have infringed upon your territory in contravention of the laws you passed but a year ago, and sire we also do not know from whence they came, so we have brought them before you so that you may pass judgement upon them."

As Nero sat upon his marble throne and surveyed the prisoners, a nubile young lady handed him a large bunch of grapes from a golden salver. As he slowly placed them one by one in his mouth he finally spoke in a rich deep sounding tone and asked, "Well then, what have you three white of skin individuals to say in your defence, and pray from whence do you come?"

Tom boldly stepped forward a pace and replied "Berkshire in Great Britain in the year 2001."

Nero suddenly roared at him, "Do you take me for a fool humble dog, it is but the year 52 and you speak of a thousand or more years hence!" then turning to the guards cried,

"Oh take the fools away and have them dismembered."

Yannie nearly wet himself with fear, so plucking up his remaining courage stepped forward and cried out, "Oh, mighty Nero, please forgive my friend over there he does not lie, we are but poor travellers from another time and we have all read about your great deeds and your fighting ability. Did I not read you were exiled here by that licentious one the other Nero?"

Then as the guards stepped forward, the reclining local Nero raised his hand and cried, "Hold, what you say stranger is true, but how you know that I know not. However, it is true I was exiled here and commanded to set up a resting place for tired Roman troops and their families to rest and take holidays. I was also instructed to provide them with other entertainments instead of the gladiator arena, and that is why my local law was passed to protect this whole area of Greece from exploitation."

Yannie quickly saw an opportunity to gain time so he quickly added, "Your very highest eminence these other three persons you see before you could be of great service to you if you spare them punishment. Between them they have untold experience in our own time because two of them run a business we call a travel agency where they arrange and sell holidays abroad in such places as here in Greece and Italy. They are also experts in how to organise accommodation and travel, therefore they could help you with your task to set up your holiday resort. Of course you could take the credit for any success of a project like that back in Rome."

Nero pondered Yannie's words for a moment as he surveyed the group of friends again, then asked them individually, "What are your names, and could you do as this dog of a slave states you can?"

Tom stepped forward again to introduce his two friends by explaining, "I am Tom this is Dick and this is Harry," as he pointed to his two mates.

Yannie, not to be excluded from the discussion remarked,

"And remember oh mighty one these men aren't any Tom Dick or Harry either! Get it?" Nero did not get the intended quip. Instead, he suddenly suggested that he would, as a concession, allow them six months to set up a so called holiday spa, and at the end of that time he would reconsider their case. Moreover, in the meantime he decreed that they would be seconded to his personal staff as advisers, along with Julius Antonius and his soothsayer Divinia Mindout.

During that period they would be fed and also enjoy all the privileges of his court; they would be temporarily raised to the rank of **consuls, paid a small salary** and afforded the services of Nymphus Cretia and her friend Ophelia Letushavit the local bordello owner.

He turned and introduced them to his adviser Julius Antonius and instructed him to have them bathed and to re-clothe them as befitting to his court, and further, that he should also introduce them to the other close members of his court.

Nero clapped his hands and dismissed them into the care of Julius Antonius, turned around and sat the young girl with the grapes on his lap encouraging her to place a ripened grape between her now naked breasts. He then, to much applause removed them one by one by mouth as she giggled uncontrollably while his other hand slid under her flimsy dress.

The four travellers, seeing his actions as they departed, began to think they might be in for a good time while setting up the proposed holiday spa, and had at that moment completely forgotten about returning back to the twenty-first century.

Julius Antonius guided the four companions towards the bath area and left them in the care of six young handmaidens. He stated that he would send his personal tailor to the bathhouse to measure them for their new clothes, and informed them his local tailor was named Hymie Greenberg, one who hailed from across the sea in Judea.

Chapter 2

The Old Shopping Mall

Inside the bathing area the wayward rugby players noticed that this particular bathhouse was so much more elegant than the previous one they had bathed at the day before.

The reason for its ornate interior, they discovered much later was because many years previously this imposing building when being constructed had imported polished marble slabs and extra ornate pillars with figures attached representing the gods spaced evenly around its outer walls. The water inside the bath area was quite hot, thanks to the many slaves stoking its underground heating arrangement. This helped it to lazily cascade over marble steps set at various heights down into the bubbling water below where it eventually settled lazily into a large ornate pool with a golden fountain set into its middle from which sprang a steamy cascade of cool scented water. This fountain had a seating area also made of glistening polished green marble, where sat sixteen nubile handmaidens awaiting their duties.

The four companions were divested of their clothing, and they quickly jumped into the pool to be instantly surrounded by young women two to each man ready to wash them and scent them before they were measured for their new clothes.

The tailor to the royal court arrived and sat on a small marble stool watching the antics of our reluctant travellers in the pool as he tried to assess their body sizes.

With them being rugby players they were all much larger in stature compared to his usual clients, then as Harry leaped up out of the water while he frolicked with two naked girls, the tailor decided there and then that he would have to make Harry's toga slightly longer than his rugby companions because his appendage did appear to be the largest.

Moreover his only view of Yannie seemed to be his rear end as he was once again practising his Greek shagging technique on one of his willing bathing companions. Tom and Dick were also sampling the hospitality of two of the girls, apparently oblivious to the crowd of onlookers.

Suddenly through an open doorway appeared an elegant very upright Roman centurion with short cut blonde hair. He had on a white toga interlaced with gold thread and sported a long gold earring in his left ear. The babble of voices in the bathhouse became quite subdued as he approached the pool area, as suddenly a voice cried out, "It is Unctuous Uranus who doth approach."

As he came nearer to the edge of the pool, he called to the four companions in a very effeminate voice, "Would you like to sample my staff you lovely boys?" To emphasise his request he lifted his toga to reveal an erect staff of some twelve inches in length.

Yannie, who at the time was bending over washing his hair, on hearing that request straightened up so quickly he nearly ricked his back. Then placing his hand discretely over his rear end stared at the centurions appendage in awe and cried in his deepest male voice, "I've seen bigger ones on Greek schoolboys, so hang a flag on it, and piss off."

Uranus just grinned, tucked his staff under his toga and cried, "See you later sweet one!" as he turned and headed back towards his abode in the local Bordello 'El' Roma' run by Ophelia Letushavit who was also watching the proceedings from the other side of the pool.

The four companions, after that interruption, had given up all thoughts about having sex and were now busily being dried off by their handmaidens ready for the attentions of their new tailor.

The tailor, Greenberg, had already left and was now awaiting them in his shop in the street of a thousand slaves named Exodus Way.

Julius Antonius returned and escorted the four companions, now already firm friends, to the tailors shop for the fitting of their new clothes. On the way he stopped and introduced them to Divinia Mindout the local soothsayer, who immediately suggested they beware the ides of March. Before they reached the tailors shop they had also met one Marcus Aborious, another adviser to Nero, also known as the most boring man in Syracuse. On their way they also had to pass the local bordello, which they quickly hurried on by as they saw Uranus eyeing them from a balcony window with a gleam in his eye.

Eventually they reached the tailor's shop where Antonius left them to be dressed while he visited the bordello for a drink, or so he professed.

Once inside the shop they found that the tailor had six assistants and there were rolls and rolls of cloth in all colours, although predominately white. Within the space of two hours, he had them all clad in respectable togas with a silk lining. Each of them also requested a small top pocket to keep their old credit cards, in which was secured by a gold laced thread for safety purposes. Each garment also had a woven, gold coloured leather belt secured to its waistband and attached to what was a small scabbard that could house a weapon of some kind. While they tried them on they congratulated the tailor on his efforts. As Julius returned from the bordello to inspect their new garments and after studying them for a while, he pronounced that he thought his master Nero would be pleased with their new look, and he would now show them to their new quarters.

After Julius had paid the tailor for his work, he escorted them to their new home in a street aptly named Greek Street which suited Yannie and his ego admirably.

The group of men arrived at their new lodgings and were greeted by one Diana Faleciana the owner, who was known locally to be rather oversexed as she was an ex Roman Goddess of love. Moreover she was a tall woman, very blonde and exceptionally big busted to say the least – Yannie estimated a 42D in modern terms.

Julius introduced the four men, then handed Diana the directive from Nero containing the terms of his agreement with her which was to house and feed the new boarders until instructed otherwise. She pressed her seal ring onto the document as Julius bid them farewell, saying he would collect them for a meeting with Nero the next day at 9am, and left the group heading for the royal courthouse.

Diana took hold of Tom and Harry placing her arm through their own and whispered "Follow me, I will show you your rooms." As they walked they could both feel the firmness of her bosoms resting on their forearms, as with each step they joggled up and down as she walked forward. Yannie, who was following behind, was admiring her rump which he could see quite clearly through her short flimsy pleated white toga. He turned to Dick and remarked,

"Some landlady this one eh mate?" Dick said nothing because his mind was racing ahead and imagining having his next breakfast in bed, with you know whom!

As they walked to their own rooms their new landlady explained her rules of the house: no lady guests whatsoever unless supplied by her, the group would be housed together two to a room and those rooms had no doors only sheepskin covers over the entrances. The bordello also had three separate bathhouses with constant hot and cold running water thanks, she added, to her two Eunuch slaves who constantly fed the underground fire that heated the water. Their beds would be simple ones made of wood and raffia with each room sporting two small wooden tables with various rugs and blankets made from sheep and goatskins. To eat their food with were basic utensils made of copper, and there were earthenware jugs holding fresh water. However, they were to provide their own wine for consumption; although the boys could buy her special brew at what she guaranteed was a bargain price.

Eventually they reached two adjacent rooms and she lifted the sheepskin door cover, ushered them inside and remarked, "Remember consuls all food is served at 7pm sharp and you must ensure your oil lamp is extinguished at 10 pm sharp, is that now understood men of another world?" as she left them for her own quarters.

Dicks, remark to the rest of them was, "Christ, did you notice the knockers on that bird you guys? That pair of beauties nearly drilled a hole in my arm, that's for sure."

Yannie piped up, "I understand she was some kind of Goddess once upon a time, and if they are all like her up in heaven, I just can't wait to die!"

"Don't forget guys if we don't ingratiate ourselves with that Nero Zero guy, we might get there earlier than intended," replied Harry, wincing at the thought.

They separated into their rooms and prepared for their evening meal. On investigating the surroundings they all found their beds quite comfortable considering what they were used to at home, while at the same time they wondered how the heck they were ever going to get out of their current predicament!

Around 7pm sharp a bell rang and a young boy of around ten years of age called out from the corridor, "Food is now served."

The quartet of friends left their rooms and headed for the dining area. On arrival they found it to be a large room with ornate pillars around its edge, with a table of solid marble set in the centre of a sunken floor. The table was surrounded by steps of stone set at different heights, decorated with blue and gold cushions.

Upon the table lay roast pig and lamb, various vegetables, large bowls of grapes and figs set in real gold dishes, plus many flagons of wine and copper goblets to drink from. There, at one end, sat Diana dressed in the flimsiest of costumes that was see-through and helped enhanced her obvious ample attributes.

"Come sit with me gentlemen," she commanded as they entered and eased their way down the ornate steps into the actual dining area.

Harry could not help remarking to his new host and landlady, "What a wonderful dining area you have here, Diana."

"Tis but a pleasant room in a modest villa that I have as my abode here guests of our leader, so I suggest you fill yourselves with food and please partake of that sparkling wine in that flagon there so you may also enjoy the forthcoming entertainment that we regularly provide here."

The boys could not wait to take their fill of all the succulent food provided, and also the wine that they began to drink in copious amounts. It wasn't long before everyone around the table was singing and laughing as the red wine took its effect.

Yannie, in the meantime, just could not take his eyes off Diana's bosom as the pair of large pear shaped objects jumped around underneath her flimsy dress as she laughed and sang with her guests.

Suddenly, Diana clapped her hands and immediately servants appeared and began to clear the table of unwanted food, she then stood up quite unsteadily and cried out, "Bring on the entertainment slaves." Immediately into the room appeared five dancing girls each dressed in only a thin see-through veil. They began to gyrate and slowly dance their way down the steps towards the centre of the room, and on arriving climbed up upon the table and began the most sensuous gyrating dance one could ever imagine. Yannie was beside himself with desire as he stared up at the pubic hair of the girls as they swirled around the tabletop above him, to music provided by three lute players and a harpist sitting behind their host on a raised dais.

Gradually the dancers became more erotic in their movements, and by now all the men were sporting erections as the dancers suddenly disrobed themselves completely and Diana was heard to cry out, "Help yourselves my friends." She cast aside her own flimsy clothing and beckoned to the two centurions who had been eating at a separate table to follow her up to a small recessed area covered with cushions, and cried, "Give it to me boys," as she lay back on the cushions while the two centurions served her one at a time, until the early hours.

In the meanwhile our intrepid travellers were doing their utmost to satisfy the hungry, nubile young dancers who to them seemed totally insatiable. Much later they sank back onto the cushions provided, exhausted with their efforts but ecstatically happy.

Then as if on command, the young girls suddenly left the room as two eunuchs arrived to clear away the debris of the evening's festivities.

Our four travellers wearily got to their feet and headed for their rooms, and as they walked past their host noticed she was being serviced for the eighth time that evening. God, thought Yannie what a place to live, who wants to go back home now he mused, London was never like this was it!

Chapter 3

The Meeting

The next morning the four friends were awakened by Diana at around 7am. She appeared as bright as a new pin as she leisurely woke them by pinching each of their appendages as she cried, "Wake up dear boys, Nero awaits your pleasure." Yannie tried to grab her under her toga, but she was much too quick for him, and mockingly remonstrated with him saying, "Another time my little friend," as she again deftly dodged his groping hands.

Later, when they had eaten and bathed, Julius arrived as promised, this time however he had a small carriage drawn by two magnificent horses with which to transport them to their meeting with his leader.

Eventually when they emerged from their lodgings he addressed them thus, "Get in," and when they were all settled inside he instructed the charioteer to proceed. During their journey he remarked how tired they all looked and suggested they partake of some extra special food so that they could get used to the normal evening activities these ancient times.

Yannie who was already half asleep again by now, whispered, "What's it called mate?"

"Arrowroot and ginger," came the reply.

"Can we stop at a market place on the way and get some, then?"

"No, if we are but one minute late it means Lastrighticus for us lot, you understand stranger?"

Yannie and the rest of them already realised the significance of that name, so vowed instead to stop off after their meeting with Senator Nero.

Within a trice they were outside Nero's palace where they alighted from their carriage and were ushered up the steps for their second meeting with him.

They found him reclining on cushions as usual, and again eating grapes fed by his favourite handmaiden. They bowed their heads as he addressed them.

"Well, is your new accommodation to your liking, and have you a plan of your ideas for me this bright and sunny Grecian morning?"

Yannie was surprised to see that Nero's handmaiden had her spare hand up inside his toga, and hoped he would not be distracted from his deliberations as he, a humble taxi driver, certainly did not fancy a visit from Lastrighticus.

Harry stood up first and addressed the emperor.

"Well, Your Eminence, we have discussed amongst ourselves how we may be able to help you in your task to set up a Holiday resort." Then turning and pointing to his two friends carried on speaking, "Here before you, you see two of my colleagues who in our life and times are what are known as travel agents, with myself being a full time Bank official.

We estimate it will cost a great deal of money to set up this resort for you and with me being a banker I have a suggestion for you on how to raise part of the money for the whole venture. First of all I would propose that you contact Rome for a shipment of Gold, secondly you can also raise local taxes by ten percent to raise additional capital. I also have a scheme where we can introduce secure banks in certain locations to hold the taxes collected. Those banks will have a new innovation of a service called, a 'Hole in the Wall'. This hole will be oblong in shape and able to accept an item known as a credit card. This card will be made of a small piece of slate or marble which will have inscribed, details of the owner and his deposit of monies in the new banking system. Then for each deposit or withdrawal you, Your Eminence, will receive in royalties 5 per cent of the transaction monies as a gratuity for granting this concession. Eventually, when these banks are built, my two friends can then set up a network of small buildings called travel agencies where your subjects and troops may reserve a holiday destination. They must pay for it in advance, which is important because you yourself will again receive a percentage of that payment for granting those rights as well.

Does that explanation clarify our suggested scheme, and also does it please Your Eminence?" he inquired, trembling slightly in case Nero rejected the proposals.

Nero suddenly stood up while his handmaiden bent down and began to gather up loose black grapes from beneath his feet.

"How much do you need for this idea of yours banker, and what do you think I may personally make out of all of these future transactions?"

Harry thought for a moment, and then said, "Much gold Your Eminence. However, we can reduce costs by having slaves do the actual building work, and I predict you will be able to repay Rome for any loan they grant you within one year, and with interest. That should ingratiate you with the other Caesar, Nero, and if my first calculations are correct you will be the richest man in the whole of this land and be able to afford everything your heart desires."

The companions stood motionless as Nero sat down again and turned to his advisers standing behind him: Marcus Aborious, Julius Antonius and Divinia Mindout his soothsayer.

The group of advisers sat there whispering together for quite some time. As the four travellers began to fidget awaiting Nero's reply, Yannie whispered to Dick, "I hope the silly sod agrees or us four are for the chop."

"Quiet," whispered a nearby guard, "the emperor is thinking and if he hears you talking it will mean a visit from you know who!"

Yannie shut up immediately as he involuntarily put his hand up to his throat and began to tremble uncontrollably so much so he began to wet himself.

Dick turned to him and whispered, "Behave yourself you Greek twit, are you trying to get us all killed?"

The advisers and Nero stopped conversing and Nero rose to his feet and approached the travellers. Then leaning forward said, "Tis agreed, this idea of yours strangers. However, I must warn you that should this project fail, you will be thrown to the lions and Lastrighticus will be four payments short in his wages. Now go and begin your work whilst I contact Rome this very month."

He turned on his heels and with a wave of his ring fingered hand, dismissed all before him.

Julius turned to the travellers and said, "Let us retire and have a drink and I shall introduce you to Ophelia Letushavit our local bordello owner who serves the best wine and food anywhere in this area."

Then as they left the scene he looked down and remarked, "Pray, who doth leave that stain upon Nero's steps?"

Yannie certainly did not answer; he was holding his appendage as he walked in front of the others trying to contain the last drops of his urine.

"This way," cried Julius pointing to a side street named Adonis Lane. "It's just along here on the right hand side," he said pointing to a brightly painted blue and gold wooden doorway with gold lettering stating, 'The

Heavenly Bar'.

He knocked loudly on the door, which was immediately opened by two huge black eunuchs and the group were ushered inside. Once in the cool interior they found sat at a roughly hewn wooden desk, a wizened old lady who said, "Where's your money then my lords?"

Julius took four small coins from a leather pouch hung around his waist and cried, "Four Quadrantes my women tis enough to pay, pray make way we need to discuss business with your mistress." The old lady squinted at the coins then put them one by one in her mouth biting each one to check its authenticity; "You may enter," she said as she pointed to a darkened corridor.

Julius said, "Follow me," as he headed down the corridor that led into a long room inside which they found a large blonde female of some 100 kilos reclining on a pile of ornate cushions. Apart from her size she was incredibly beautiful. She had long, flowing blonde hair and her breasts were, as Yannie later put it, gargantuan at least 56 inches was to understate her actual size.

"What can I do for you Julius, my lovely one?" she whispered.

"We just came in for but a drink, and a snack of sorts, can you accommodate us?"

"I certainly can," she replied eyeing up his four companions. "Would you care for goats' milk laced with some fine wine and cheese that has been steeped in a few secret ingredients plus some bread?"

"That will do me," said Yannie.

"Suits us three as well," came a comment from Tom.

Their new host stood up from her resting place, clapped her hands and gave orders to two smaller coloured slaves to bring in the beverages and food.

Harry couldn't help noticing that as she clapped her hands her two breasts jiggled around like a rugby ball after

34

a goal kick. In fact, he mused, they actually looked just like two rugby balls inside an outsize bra.

When the food arrived Julius began to explain to their hostess the task they had to carry out as agreed with Nero and asked if she thought she could help them in any way concerning future entertainment facilities. She leaned forward towards the table where her ample attributes lay upon the tabletop and began to resemble two whales on heat as they protruded from the top of her flimsy dress.

Yannie was beginning to get horny again as he stared incredulously at the mountain of flesh just a few inches from his nose. Tom put a restraining hand on his leg and whispered, "Hold on you randy Greek sod I know what you're thinking, business comes first."

Their hostess for the morning sat and thought for a while at the same time fingering the long pearl necklace that cascaded down between the two mountains of her breasts. Then she spoke.

"Pray what do I receive for my efforts Julius if I agree to partake in this venture?"

"You, my lovely, will be afforded the title of Senior Administrator and also receive a percentage of the takings instead of a remuneration. You will also work closely with these four strangers who have been commanded to complete this project within six months."

Ophelia pondered for a moment as she eyed up the group sitting opposite her, then replied, "Right then I accept. When do we commence?"

Julius looked at Tom for an indication. Tom thought for a moment then said, "Actually it depends on Nero receiving confirmation from the Senate in Rome, however we could begin right away building a couple of banks using money from the local treasury. That's if you sanction it first, Julius, and I presume money therein has been collected as taxes?"

"I doth know of two scribes who can draw plans and who can write, also who we could use to draw up the building details. They are the brothers Quintillian who will do anything I ask of them!" replied Julius rather pompously. "With that settled then, I will return to Nero and put in motion all that is needed. In the meantime would you, Ophelia, keep these men amused until I return," he suggested as he rose to leave.

"Certainly I shall Your Eminence," replied Ophelia standing up and removing her flimsy gown. Looking at the group of strangers, she whispered "Who's first then?" as she lay back upon the cushions with her legs set at forty-five degrees. Immediately Yannie lifted his toga and was soon like a rabbit at a rabbits' orgy. Tom started to laugh at the sight of his tiny bottom bouncing up and down, and his head that had now almost disappeared completely between those two huge breasts as he gasped for air.

It wasn't long before the four travellers had had their fill of her wonderful body. They had covered most of her breasts with their own secretions, which she was slowly rubbing into her lily white skin as she tried to revive Yannie for the third time, unfortunately for her, without success.

Dick was beginning to enjoy his new clothing. He thought, great, no buttons or flys, no zips, just lift up and go. What a way to live, he thought, for the time being forgetting all about his wife back home in England.

Ophelia suddenly stood up, leisurely brushed her ample golden pubic hair with an ornate hand brush, then put on her gown, clapped her hands, and when two slaves arrived, ordered food for herself and her new found partners.

Later after they had eaten, Julius returned and stated that all was in place for them to proceed with their project. At the same time they agreed to rent a large room at

Ophelia's house to be set aside for their meetings and used as a place for the two scribes to draw up the building plans.

Yannie thought that this was a great idea as he had stirrings in his loins again as he stared at his host's breasts while he consumed the last of his wine.

Julius then suggested that the strangers to his land immediately draw a schedule of work so that he could regularly inform Nero of their progress. That would then allow him to instigate a payment scheme to pay the builders and obtain extra wooden tokens for the many slaves to be employed, entitling them to extra food for their labours.

Tom suggested that with Julius being a trusted aide to Nero, he himself would handle the payment record-keeping in conjunction with Ophelia, so that any auditors sent from Rome would be satisfied with the accounts. With that settled they closed the meeting and headed for the local bathhouse to refresh themselves.

Chapter 4

Progress of sorts

We now move on some three months, and during that time quite a lot of progress had been made with the building of the new banks and setting up of health spas in such places as, Piraeus, Salimus, Sikyon, Kirrha, and the farthest one being set out at Thermopylai.

Julius was so pleased with the building progress that he authorised double rations for all slaves and their offspring. Meanwhile Tom was having great difficulty with his intended 'credit card' manufacture especially when trying to reduce their size in marble to make them easily manageable. However, he eventually settled for having them made out of small pieces of onyx, in green for standard cards, and for the Roman elite, gold coloured onyx with that version including a Roman crest of Caesar upon its face side.

Harry and Dick had managed so far to complete five health spas. Each of these had a communal bathhouse, with heated water for the winter months and a dining area large enough to seat one hundred troops and their families. Each room in the individual complexes could house six adults. The builders had added to each one, after much pressure from Julius, a special 'orgy' room for any late night entertainment that may be required.

Yannie had spent most of his time running errands for his three former passengers and trying to satisfy Letushavit, he was also now so suntanned he was forever being mistaken for a slave. His three companions were, by contrast, now much leaner and fitter men, bronzed by the sun and also having had their surplus weight removed by nightly exercises with Ophelia and her best friend Nymphus Cretia a well-known oversexed retired female goddess.

Dick began to think he was actually in love with her, but was constantly reminded by the others when bouts of their memory returned, about his charming wife back in the twenty-first century. That, however, did not stop him drooling over her body, as she was his favourite type of woman. Pure blonde with long golden tresses, and almost six feet in height, she also sported beautiful up tilting breasts that resembled two large lemons. Her waist was only 20 inches in circumference and down below that, her pubic hair was so fine it felt like baby down to the touch.

Later that morning Julius wandered by and suggested they all convene for a meeting so that he could give Nero a progress report, as they were now half way through his original time limit of six months. He also needed to send a report to Rome detailing their expenditure to date.

He also suggested that for a change they meet in a bar in Greek Street where he had had a room set aside that was soundproof, and he would provide two mute guards to ensure no one overheard their deliberations. So it was agreed they would all meet the next day, and Julius would also supply two scribes to record the facts and figures so that Nero II could inform Rome of their progress.

Julius then left them to arrange the venue for the meeting Tom Dick and Harry decided to spend the rest of the day gathering the information regarding their own efforts over the past three months to present a report to him the next day at their meeting.

Yannie was delegated to ensure that they weren't

interrupted in their deliberations, and also to guarantee they all had a quiet night so that they would be fresh for the following morning.

"Does that mean no sex tonight then?" he moaned.

"Yes it does," replied Tom in an exasperated tone, dismissing him with a wave of his hand. Dick and Harry smiled to themselves as they picked up their quill pens to begin their task.

Chapter 5

The Interim Report

Next morning Yannie woke the other three as agreed because he had been awakened some time earlier having booked an early call by a young nubile nymph all of 16 years of age. He had slept naked so that she could have a glimpse of his appendage, but he was rather disappointed when she just grinned at him as he stood before her naked putting on his toga. What he didn't know was that she was a prodigy of Unctuous Uranus, a royal guard to Nero who was as bent as a rusty nail, but sported a huge piece of equipment underneath his toga.

Later, after eating a hearty breakfast, the four companions hired a cart drawn by an old donkey to convey them to the meeting place; having first of all tied together their mountain of paperwork which Tom took control of as he sat at the back of the cart complaining about odd bits of straw sticking in his bottom.

"We must do something about providing a better transport service than this, don't you think?" he said turning to Dick. Before he could answer Yannie piped up, "Now you're talking boys, and I am just the man to run it don't you think? Especially with my ten years taxiing experience."

Harry pulled him up close to his own face and glared at him and said, "Well, you little Greek prat, if we ever let you run the business just you make sure there are no funny straps in them, because it's your bloody fault we are all here in the first place."

Dick then decided to speak up as well, "Perhaps that might be the way back home chaps, you know red straps and all that, what do you think?"

"We will just have to wait and see. This Nero guy might have us executed anyway if he doesn't like the results of our holiday spa scheme, so let's put that idea on hold for the time being, right?" Tom replied.

The cart eventually pulled up at the end of Greek Street and the companions alighted having paid the driver two Quadrans for his trouble about one pence in their own time. The group then made their way to the meeting place suggested by Julius, that was a room set at the back of a wine bar called The Aqua Rest, located but a few yards away.

As they arrived outside and were about to enter Divinia Mindout the soothsayer walked passed them crying 'Beware the ides of March'. Silly cow, thought Yannie it's only June so what's she on about. Apparently he had never read anything about ancient Rome.

They entered the bistro to be met by Julius who was accompanied by two huge guards. He gave a clenched fist sign and they both immediately stood to attention either side of a roughly hewn wooden door, that led to a small room lit by two oil lamps stood upon a table set for six people. The two scribes who accompanied him he also ushered into the room.

"Good morning comrades" he cried as they all sat around the large table, "I have just ordered refreshment to be brought to us in one hour's time, so shall we proceed with the meeting men?"

The two scribes sat at a small table to the rear of the group with their quill pens to the ready as the meeting began.

Tom unrolled their paperwork and proceeded to act as

spokesperson as he gave the following progress report: First and foremost his two colleagues had already set up and established six health spas at different places on the coast line, such as Megara and Eleusis and these had also been built ahead of schedule and well within their budgeted cost. He then leaned over closer to Julius and whispered, "You could share in that saving if you so wish?"

Julius's face lit up as he nodded his agreement, and called to the scribes to delete that last statement from the records.

Tom carried on detailing all that had happened to date including the setting up of the six banks. He then reported he was still having difficulty with the new credit cards and especially the manufacture of the slotted tubes to carry them into the bank for verification before any cash could be drawn, and that statement would end his report.

Julius stated he would visit the manufacturers personally, and should the problems not be resolved within the next half moon appearing, they would receive a visit from one, Lastrighticus.

The meeting was then concluded, and the scribes were instructed to complete their reports by the morrow so that they could be presented to Nero. Julius decided to go to the nearest bank with Tom to collect his share of the construction savings, and a smaller share for his boss Nero. His decision, if later revealed, would result in his immediate demise but the thought of all those Aureus gold coins enhancing his secret cache of money overrode his fear of a visit by Lastrighticus.

A few days later he visited his Senator, Nero II and presented him with his three-monthly report. On the senator's acceptance he slid a leather bag containing a large sum of gold coins across the table and whispered, "Your share of the strangers' savings on the building costs so far, Your Eminence."

Nero slid the bag into his own hand and gave it a squeeze, and remarked, "More to come I hope Julius my trusted friend."

Julius Antonius replied in the affirmative before bidding his master farewell as he left to visit the wayward manufacturers of the credit card tubes.

Meanwhile Tom, Dick, Harry and Yannie where heading for Ophelia Letushavit the local bordello owner to discuss the entertainments programme for the combined opening nights of the holiday spas scheduled for the following month of July.

The group, after arriving at the bordello, had a small meal and then sat around a large wooden table discussing the forthcoming openings, and advancing their ideas about entertainment.

Yannie was the first to suggest a Gladiatorial orgy live on a stage, with real Roman gladiators dragging what would appear unwilling naked girls into a fake arena, where they would squeeze over ripe grapes over their naked bodies before having sex with them. Divinia immediately pooh- poohed that idea saying that was a once a week scene anyway, and would probably cause little interest. However, she had an idea of her own that involved the following people some of whom the strangers had not met as yet and she listed them before explaining her idea. First she named All-Alonis, an old Greek god who she knew as a lonely lover, then Unctuous Uranus the big queer guard, also one Aquas Erectus a horny master slave and last but not least Sinus Conquerus a legendary Roman lover. Then she added as an afterthought, those men I have named are all how we say in Greece, well different to most other men. Yannie couldn't help piping up with, "Sounds like a load of queers to me mates?"

"So what, we could have fun choreographing that lot

couldn't we boys?" Tom muttered turning to the others.

"Agreed," cried Dick and Harry in unison while Harry added, "It's about time we did something different, and I'd love to see those silly sods stuck into their new task."

"Shall we agree a price for their services then, and I would suggest two Sesterlus or Denarius's each for a two hour performance and if you gentlemen agree, I will arrange the details with Unctuous Uranus during the next week?"

The rest of the group nodded in agreement, and went on to discuss ideas about other forms of entertainment. Eventually after much mind searching, they came up with a complete programme for the opening night and it was further agreed they would put this final list to Julius Antonius for approval.

Divinia stood up and announced, "Well how about a short session, you men, in my bathhouse before you leave?"

Yannie was so eager to be first he immediately jumped up from the table, unfortunately catching his little willy on the rough hewn wood and obtaining a splinter in you know where. He hopped around holding his appendage as the others fell about laughing. However, later he didn't mind when Divinia decided to suck out the offending splinter, in fact much later he left the bordello with a big smile on his face as the group headed for another meeting with Antonius after he returned with his report regarding the manufacture of the tubing for the new credit cards.

Meanwhile, being quite clever, Julius had easily resolved the problem when he suggested that the new cards should be made into an oval shape, this would allow them to turn any corners or negotiate any kinks in the tubing manufacture. That little suggestion cost all of the three manufactures twenty gold Aureus, after mentioning the name of the executioner, with no receipts given. As he headed back to his meeting with the wayward travellers he smiled to himself and mused, thank you for your backing Lastrighticus my old friend!

Chapter 6

The Credit Card Tryout

Julius had met the others later that same day and agreed the opening programme for the entertainments. He also urged them to chase the completion of the last two banks and he thought that it should be easy now that he had personally solved the credit card problem. He went on to suggest, and eventually got an agreement from them, to raise his share of the anti, from 5 to 7 percent. Tom didn't argue he was going to do the books anyway wasn't he!

Julius left again to report to Nero on their progress including the expected opening dates of the banks and the spas. However, on the way he decided not to mention the kind of entertainment planned for the openings at that stage because he thought his centurion master would enjoy watching something new and if gently pressed maybe partake in the ceremony himself.

That evening Tom and Dick heard Yannie moaning in his room so they went along to investigate. They found Yannie with his toga up around his waist sitting on his bed trying to push small wooden splinters into his willy. However, he found it much too painful to endure as obviously he had been hoping, should he achieve his bizarre aims, that Divinia would later be on hand to administer her sucking technique again.

Tom and Dick burst out laughing as they entered the room, because Yannie jumped when they entered and slid forward crushing his somewhat tender private parts on the edge of the rough-hewn plank of wood surrounding his bed.

"Christ, you two frightened the life out of me, why didn't you knock?"

"What, on a bloody sack, you silly Greek sod, and stop playing with yourself you are much too old for that caper!" Tom shouted at him.

"I wasn't playing with myself, you rugby twit, I was only trying to clean up my poor wound."

"And pigs still fly do they, come off it Yannie," cried Dick.

His two friends ushered him out of the room as they informed him they were to attend the testing of the credit cards at the largest bank accompanied by Divinia, Julius and Harry. Their first appointed bank manager was to be one Sinus Timorous a local candidate who was the wimpiest of the local civil servants and had been specially selected by Tom and Julius. Those two were no fools, because the two of them would need to dominate him so that the skimming of monies for themselves would be that much easier.

The bank itself was situated in a street named 'Needle-thread Street' as most of the other small businesses operating there were in the rag trade.

The group strode through the morning sunshine towards the bank as once again Divinia the local soothsayer strolled past crying out, "Beware the ides of April!"

Yannie couldn't help himself, "Now its April is it, instead of March? What's the old girl on about now or is she on Eastern Time or something, because she's now 3 months behind the old boot?"

Dick shouted, "Leave it out Yannie she quite harmless, well unless of course you are resident in Rome and a Senator."

The group arrived at the bank at that same moment as Julius with the selected bank manager who was a thin weedy looking individual. Also attending were a few other friends including Antonius Ophelia Letushavit and Nymphus Cretia.

When Yannie saw the two females side by side he began to have carnal thoughts again. He began leering like a schoolboy until Tom gave him a poke in the back reminding him the meeting was strictly business and the women were only sleeping partners in the business sense that was!

The little bank manager opened the door with a large key while two huge guards stood either side of him and once the group were inside its cool interior Julius gleefully pointed out the credit card desk. It was made from a highly polished slab of marble, with two polished channels cut into the centre, one with the word engraved in gold 'In' and the other 'Out'. The tube stating 'Out' had a smaller tube set about two feet above the other one. Julius then explained that when the new two part oval credit card arrived down the first tube, the bank clerk would verify the owner's identity by comparing his 'mark' against a master copy of it held in a tray on his right hand side. Then after verification he would authorise withdrawal and record the details of the transaction in the bank's log book. He would then pass the card to his colleague, who in turn would place the selected amount of monies inside the card, lock it together and place it in the upper tube then ring a bell to indicate the transaction was completed. Below the bank in a cellar, a specially selected team of slaves would start pumping on a pair of large leather bellows that would force air down the tube and propel the card and monies to its owner waiting outside the bank at the tubes' exit point.

Yannie was sent outside with a sample credit card to try out the system and he couldn't wait to prove the system couldn't work. Moreover much to everybody's surprise, it worked without a hitch, to much hand clapping from those present. Julius and Tom decided that to prevent any fraud that would reduce their own percentage, they would secretly have a word with Lastrighticus to have a little chat with all new recruited credit card staff. He would explain their responsibilities including their loss of pension rights and probably their heads as well, if they so much as made just one double entry or withdrawal either by mistake or on purpose.

With the demonstration over, Dick and Harry were asked to check the other new banks' systems before the grand opening of all the branches and the spas in September in the year 52. Meanwhile, Yannie already had his hand up Nymphus Cretia's flimsy skirt anticipating a little favour later in the day, however much to his surprise he found her private parts locked into a golden type chastity belt that felt extremely hot to his touch. She looked down at him and remarked, "You find the key little man and I shall be all yours later."

Yannie spent the rest of the day searching Ophelia's bordello without any success whatsoever. Little did he realise that the key to her golden crumpet was a special poem to be whispered in her ear that had been her punishment by the Gods for her previous indiscretions.

Ophelia wasn't going to let him into the secret yet as she had ideas of her own about him. She liked little men at times because she could smother them with her ample charms and soft warm body, and she secretly hoped he would pick up another splinter you know where!

Meanwhile, Dick and Harry had headed off for the other banks to check the card system, whilst Tom and Julius headed for a local bar for a drink and to discuss the final report to Nero.

Chapter 7

Banks and Spas Opening Day

Over the last month the whole group of friends had been busy checking and re-checking the holiday spas and the banks, and reviewing the arrangements for the opening entertainments show. During that period the temperature had been in the 25 Celsius range every day, giving our rugby players a hard time especially having no sun-blocker. Ophelia helped solve the problem by rubbing olive oil into their burnt skin every evening, then rubbing copious amounts onto her own body, before encouraging them to do their worst to her ever willing body.

Yannie, during that time, had been put in charge of dress rehearsals for the opening show, and had quickly learnt not to bend down at anytime when Unctuous Uranus was performing. He still couldn't get over the length of the Royal guards appendage as he rehearsed with his queer partners dressed in gear designed by Nymphus Cretia. The gear consisted of black leather straps studded with gold buttons which were strapped tightly around their arms, legs and buttocks, with a cod piece with a hole in the front to let their ample equipment poke through for use at the finale of the show.

He watched as the men on stage enacted a gladiatorial fight, cavorting about all around the stage that now represented a Roman arena. It was soon obvious whom the victor would be, one Unctuous Uranus. He gradually eliminated all of the other gladiators in turn and finally, as the last one succumbed to his mighty sword play, he tore aside his protagonist's leather thong and entered him from behind, to raucous cheers from the rest of the cast of the show.

Yannie was amazed that not one whimper of pain emanated from the fallen gladiator but he did assume that it was a case of 'practice makes perfect'. He signalled to the producer that he approved of the final scene, then made his mark on the official agreement form, which would guarantee the participants full pay and maybe a bonus if Nero II also approved of their performance on the night.

He then decided to head back to his quarters and report to the others his opinion of the forthcoming show with the firm conviction that none of them should ever, ever bend over in the presence of the tall skinny Uranus. Even his own name was to put it mildly, too close for comfort of his favourite human hobby site.

He arrived back with the others just after noon and it was decided by all of them that due to the oppressive heat they should discuss the last details of the opening day in the coolness of a communal bathhouse. Julius led the way, followed by Nymphus Cretia and Ophelia cavorting about naked on the way there, with our four lost friends in hot pursuit and Yannie after his episode at rehearsals ready for anything, or for that matter, anybody!

Later that afternoon, there was much frivolity between the whole ensemble that included an exhibition of her sexual prowess by Nymphus, who not only seduced all and sundry there but finished off the afternoon in a sixty-nine configuration with Ophelia, to more resounding cheers from the onlookers.

The whole group decided that from then until the opening day which was set for the forthcoming Saturday, they should rest, eat well and sleep well. Of course our intrepid, unwilling travellers were not used to all the shenanigans in ancient Greece and really needed all the rest they could get.

Finally, the Saturday opening day arrived, and everyone awoke to brilliant sunny weather including a cooling breeze. Harry thought that ought to help him and his companions cope with the day's exertions, especially the travel between the spas and banks checking that things were going to plan, and praying that their new adopted master Nero II would approve of the whole set-up, and maybe reward them accordingly!

Then for a moment or two, he thought of Britain in the twentieth century and offered up a small prayer for a solution and their return home. Dick as he was finishing his morning breakfast asked, "What you thinking about mate, getting back home again because so was I?"

"Funny, I was thinking just that very same thing myself," remarked Tom. "Anyway something will turn up, it always does you know!"

"I wouldn't mind staying here a while longer though, because my old woman back home is always on to me, nagging all the time, she is, about who I might have slept with and me just a hard working taxi driver doing sixteen hours a day." Remarked Yannie wistfully.

Later that morning the group of friends accompanied by Ophelia and Nymphus Cretia climbed into a large hired chariot and headed off towards the venue for the opening ceremony at Piraeus the nearest spa. At the same time Nero was leaving his palace surrounded by centurion guards in chariots and also accompanied by six handmaidens. He looked resplendent in his gold breastplate and finest silk toga embroidered with myths of ancient Greece, and along side of him was his trusted aide Julius.

Later at the spa both sets of travellers arrived at the same time, and where Julius had previously arranged a small feast for all the guests and the cast of the opening play.

The group of guests sat around a long wooden table on their haunches, whilst Nero reclined on a raised marble dais supported by large cushions in many colours with three hand maidens on each side of him to attend his every need.

Later after they had all eaten and partaken of much wine, Julius informed everybody that the opening ceremony was scheduled for around four pm, just before dusk, and the entertainment show would commence after Nero had performed the opening ceremony.

The whole entourage then proceeded towards the spa gates where the centurions had to force their way through the hundreds of peasants and slaves jostling for a view of their leader Nero II.

When he arrived at the gates he found them bedecked with golden painted leaves that Tom in his infinite wisdom had originally suggested might impress their host Nero. Julius pushed his way to the front of the crowd while the guards pushed our lost rugby chums, including the two lady charmers, to the front of the crowd.

When the five men including Ophelia and Nymphus Cretia were at the front, Julius asked the guards to form a half circle around him and the others, and then turning to Nero recanted the following: "Your Royal Eminence it is our most gracious pleasure to afford you the honour of opening this newly formed spa and internal banking facility for the use of your own and the troops of Rome. It is befitting that the generosity of Rome and your good self has made this all possible; with may I add the help of these strangers you see before you. Therefore it would give us all great pleasure if you were to cut the golden ribbon adorning these two gates."

Nero stepped forward and removed his own sword

from the scabbard around his waste and cut through the ribbon, to a tumultuous cheers from the assembled crowds.

Two huge slaves immediately opened the carved wooden gates set with cast bronze hinges, and allowed him to enter first accompanied by his friends and half of the centurion guard's, whilst the rest of his guards kept the crowd outside the new facility.

As the entourage strolled towards the first accommodation block, they stopped outside the newly constructed bank, where it was suggested by Julius, that Nero try out his personal gold credit card. Nero pulled the card from a pouch at his side and opened it by turning it half way, placed a copper marker inside denoting that he required six Aureus coins, then slid it into the slot marked (CCO) in Latin meaning credit cards only. A few moments later his credit card returned via the (CCCT) slot, denoting credit card completed transaction, also in Latin.

On opening it up he found inside the requested amount of coinage, and was utterly delighted. Julius reported to all those present, especially Tom, that he had to modify the whole scheme in a hurry because of problems with certain size of money bags becoming stuck in the tubes. This way the amount drawn was restricted to what the card could physically hold, and would give the bank time to send a runner to the card holders' main bank, should they wish to draw monies from a different bank. He also stated that the users of the other card, the Green one, would be smaller in size reflecting the owners' reduced spending power.

He then turned to his leader and informed him that he had issued instructions that should any of the new banking staff divulge the details of any person's card, or in anyway attempt to defraud the bank of monies, one Lastrighticus, without trial, would summarily execute them.

While strolling on towards the entertainments hall,

Nero began congratulating his visitors on their fulfilment of their programme promise and suggested he would contact Rome and see if one of their greatest philosophers could help them in their request to return to their own time. In the meantime he would grant them all centurion status in his court, and further provide extra finances to up-grade their hotel accommodation with one Diana Faleciana. In future they would be granted freedom to purchase any items on his own charge account, except his new credit card!

The group of friends wisely thanked him profusely for his new favours to them, and prayed that someone in Rome could help solve their return to Britain in the year 2001. Meanwhile they intended to enjoy every minute of their enforced stay in ancient Greece.

By this time the group had reached the entertainments centre and on entering they found themselves at one the end of a very large hall, with rows of oak seats and the walls were decorated with silken drapes that seemed to impress Nero immediately.

He was ushered to his reserved seat at the front with Julius and three of his guards and two handmaidens. Tom, Dick Harry and Yannie took their sets behind him, as the rest of the group arranged themselves behind them in a hubbub of noisy anticipation awaiting the beginning of the show.

Julius shouted, "Quite everyone," then clapped his hands for the show to start. Yannie having already seen the opening at the dress rehearsal decided he would attempt to grope one of Nero's handmaidens from behind in the semi darkness.

On the stage in front of the audience, lit by five large oil lamps was a scene depicting a Roman gladiatorial arena. Suddenly from out of what appeared a steel cage appeared four men dressed as gladiators, to be followed, to riotous cheers, by none other than Unctuous Uranus, one of Nero's favourite guards, sporting an already enormous erection.

Yannie, meanwhile, hesitated for a second or two as he slid his podgy little hand under the ever-willing buttocks of a blonde handmaiden hoping against hope she would not alert Nero. Yannie valued of all things his little willy, but most of all his curly head.

What then followed up on the stage amazed Dick and Harry; however Tom had been to Amsterdam on business and witnessed similar goings on in a gay nightclub. After about an hour that part of the show was eventually over to much applause from the Roman guards and Nero. That scene was then followed by six dancing girls doing a form of striptease to music played by a harpist. Julius had to restrain some of Nero's guards from attempting to rush the stage and join in on the girl's act. They sat extremely quietly when at the corner of the stage they suddenly spotted a giant of a man, Lastrighticus.

Julius turned to his guests and whispered, "That is him, Lastrighticus, yes the big man in the corner over there."

Yannie's hand went cold as he began to shiver on hearing the news, but couldn't remove it from the young lady's bottom as she had it securely trapped by her hairy mound.

Tom leaned towards him and whispered, "For Christ's sake Yannie behave yourself, we can't go home without you, especially if you are headless you silly prat."

Yannie didn't answer as he was now ogling the girls on the stage and imagining he was up there giving his own performance. Suddenly he jumped as the young handmaiden in front reached behind, grabbed his erect member and proceeded to masturbate him.

Diana and Ophelia were also in their own little world

as they kissed in the darkness and fondled each other. The rest of the audience were so engrossed with the action on stage they were oblivious to what was going on right under their noses.

When eventually the show was over and the invited crowd began to disperse, Nero invited the three rugby players and Yannie to a feast at his local palace back in Athinai much later that evening. As he was leaving with his guards beckoned to Ophelia and suggested she and her friend also join him at the feast, then he departed to a fanfare of trumpets.

The four travellers and the two women climbed into their waiting chariot, gave the driver a small gratuity and suggested he hurry back as they felt that a bath before the forth coming feast began would help freshen them up for the evening's festivities.

Chapter 8

The Feast

Later that same day after arriving back at Diana's place which was their original lodging house, she had her slaves stoke up the boiler so that the lads could take their bath. After all it was a hot and dusty ride especially in an open topped chariot.

The boys quickly stripped off in their rooms and headed to the bath area where they found Diana waiting with fresh scented towelling and a large flagon of wine at her side.

"Come my lovely ones, I have added some special ingredients into the water that should help relax and excite you all, and if you so wish I can join you in the water later?" she added with a wicked smile on her face.

Yannie was already ahead of her as he sported an erection under cover of the blue coloured water. Tom suggested to the others that he thought they had achieved a great deal in the last six months, and perhaps they should take up Nero's suggestion that he contact a Roman sage who might then be able to help them return home, because lately he was losing sleep at night wondering about his family. Dick and Harry also agreed, however Yannie seemed pre-occupied with his own thoughts at that particular moment.

Suddenly Diana re-appeared in the bathhouse accompanied by Nymphus Cretia and Ophelia LetusHavit, each and every one of them completely naked. Diana cried out, "Well my lovely lodgers who' first then?"

Although the lads were tired with all their efforts of late, they could not resist an offer like that, as they each selected one woman then started to perform. Yannie turned to the three women and cried, "What about poor old me then!"

Ophelia looked over her shoulder, as she was being serviced by Tom and retorted, "In a little while my small one, just be patient," she said with a gasp as Tom exploded inside of her.

Tom stood down as did Dick and Harry from their respective love goddesses, because they all found having sex in the bath was actually quite exhausting. Yannie tried to run through the water towards his chosen woman and slipped on the soap and ended up with his head jammed between Ophelia's more than ample bosom, as Diana sunk her very sharp teeth into his appendage and began to extract his love juice. His three companions stood in the warm water laughing as he tried to extricate himself from her grasp, whilst her other companion Nymphus held him in place with a finger stuck in you know where.

Eventually they released him and the group left the warmth of the bathing area to prepare themselves for the evenings visit to Nero's palace for the forthcoming feast.

Just before they left the lodgings, the tailor Hymie Greenberg called by and informed them he had been commissioned to manufacture more new clothing befitting them becoming centurions. He then asked, what Yannie considered the stupidest question ever, which was, "Which side do you dress boys?"

What a prat he thought, does it matter when you aren't wearing any underwear? However the tailor explained that their new dress uniform had an enclosed bottom area, hence his original question. Having received and logged their individual answers he left to start his work.

When he heard the tailors explanation, Yannie thought, at last no more chaffed bottoms for us, well except for having a bit of nooky on the hard stone beds. The thought took him back to when he and his family had visited Pompeii in Italy whilst on holiday some years ago, and their guide for the day had gleefully pointed out the worn out sleeping areas in the local bordellos of the day.

In another room and when they were all ready, the three women presented themselves to our four travellers, and as Tom remarked at the time they all looked absolutely fabulous dressed in all white diaphanous, clinging, see-through material, that showed every part of their attributes to good effect.

They all left the boarding house arm in arm to walk the few hundred yards to Nero's palace, where on arrival they were greeted by Julius and All Alonis a deposed Greek god, who kept giving Yannie sidelong glances. He was also accompanied by one Marco Gigolo an out of favour womanising male god, and viewed by many as an Adonis because of his looks and his Herculean figure.

When the greetings were over Julius led them to their seats set on the far end of the same table where Nero sat resplendent in an all silk golden toga. He waved to them, indicating they should sit down, then clapped his hands and gave an order for the feast to commence.

The whole area became a hive of activity as hordes of slaves brought in food stacked on silver trays. The food consisted of roasted pig, goat and lamb: each was a whole beast that the slaves were just able to carry to the table.

Each person in turn cut flesh from the roasted animals with sharp knives provided by their host, one to each guest the vegetables were so abundant that the table groaned under their weight and these were then handed to the guests by young female servants dressed in little more than a string of beads. There was also much frivolity as these young ladies leaned over to pass around the food, as the men guests were forever fondling their ample, if almost too young, charms.

Much later, after the guests had all eaten their fill, Julius, raising his voice above the hubbub of voices, announced that Nero wished to make a speech as he thundered on the table to be heard.

Nero then stood up, rather unsteadily and mainly the worse for drink. He just stood there swaying as he surveyed his audience for a minute or two, then he spoke the following words.

"Friends, Romans, Greeks and our guests from over the sea. I would like to express my thanks to the strangers in our midst for the setting up of the holiday spas, on time and within my budget, and also the setting up of the new banking system. That should prove as invaluable and also incorruptible service thanks to Lastrighticus over there," indicating his executioner who was polishing his sword.

"I have also this day sent a courier to Rome to inquire if we may assist our guests to return whence they came. However, in the meantime I have by decree enrolled them as centurions on my Royal staff, and they are to be afforded the same rights as all centurions under the command of Rome." Then turning to Julius, commanded him to bring forth his decree document for him to place his seal upon the parchment, which Julius did dutifully perform.

He then sat down and signalled for the music and the entertainment to begin, whilst the slaves hurriedly cleared away all the dirty dishes, at the same time and brushing the dropped food from the ornate marble floor, as the guests prepared to enjoy themselves even further.

For the rest of that evening the guests enjoyed the antics of court jesters and Grecian Roman wrestling where many bets were placed. The final act of the evening was a horde of naked girls dancing and cavorting about in enticing and suggestive poses, to even more raucous cheers from the men in the audience. Nero was indicating to Julius on a slate tablet his selection of girls from the performing troupe for an all night orgy at his palace, which he then handed to Julius to action.

The lads from Britain decided to leave early after seeking Nero's permission, and they and their three women companions left arm in arm, rather unsteadily, and headed for the lodging house run by Diana. On the way Nymphus Cretia suggested they all stop off on the way at Ophelia's place for a late night drink to which they all readily agreed; Yannie was already half erect in anticipation of a night with his favourite goddess's.

When they arrived at the bordello Ophelia suggested they might as well all spend the night at her place, so she despatched a runner to inform the eunuchs at the lodging house to lock up for the night, and the others would be back for breakfast the following morning.

With this chore settled Ophelia requested her slaves to prepare a large hot bath for them all and had three flagons of red wine placed around the bathing area for them to partake of. They all undressed and jumped into the hot scented water to the sounds of a lyre playing a romantic melody, whilst two young slaves handed goblets of red wine to them one at a time. Most of this wine ended up over Diana and Nymphus more than ample bosoms to be consumed by a rampant young Greek, named Yannie.

Around two a.m. they all climbed from the warm water shattered by their efforts, while the three women smiled at each other having been partially satisfied. Ophelia had arranged for the men to have a relaxing massage before going to bed, and this was carried out on each individual by well-trained, nymph like young girls around the age of sixteen. Then, even when covered in sweet smelling massage oil and with the young ladies fingers dancing over their bodies, not one of the men could rise to a further occasion. When their individual massages were complete they took to their beds and immediately fell asleep, whilst their hosts spent another hour or two giving each other intimate pleasures.

Chapter 9

Yannie and a brilliant New Idea

After their night out at Nero's party and their all night stay at the bordello, our group of unwilling travellers awoke tired and very hungry. However this was soon taken care of by Ophelia who had laid on a most lavish breakfast pick-me-up for them. They each sat down to fresh oysters caught locally, or fairly locally as their host later informed them. She had also provided cool asses' milk and varied fruits to nourish their tired bodies, and for once she did not offer them any personal favours. She thought to herself poor souls they look so tired and hoped that time permitting she could eventually get them up to the normal Roman sexual standard, especially where stamina was concerned.

When the men had eaten they decided to visit the new banks they had created and find out how business was progressing. Tom suggested they go alone, as he didn't trust Julius one hundred percent not to inform on their activities secretly to Nero II.

The group set off for the nearest bank with Yannie driving a hired chariot, because the one promised by Nero had yet to materialise in their new found, roles as centurions.

On reaching the bank, Tom and the others approached Sinus Timorous and asked to see his financial books. He immediately took them through into an inner room guarded by two huge eunuchs, where he opened the books up for scrutiny by Tom. As Tom came from a banking environment he quickly ascertained that for the short time the bank had been open, large profits were already being generated.

He then decided that the group share should be increased after he noticed that Julius had already amassed a large account for himself when he had, without discussing with his colleagues carried out his modification of the credit cards. It was also clear he was creaming money from the manufacturers in what was then termed Roman royalties. Tom requested that for a regular fee that his appointed manager one Sinus Timorous should slightly alter his books and those of all the other banks regarding the amount he actually put through the books. Timorous was delighted to oblige as he was in the process of building his own villa somewhere near the new spa at Piraeus, and that extra money would certainly allow him to use real marble for his bathing area.

Yannie decided to ask a question at that stage, so lowering his voice asked, "How are we going to horde our share Tom, it could be worth far more back home?"

"I suggest we accept the money in Aureus, then have them melted down here in secret, then Timorous here can have them made into jewellery or ornaments. That way if we ever get out of this place they could be worth a small fortune, and all we should receive in ready cash is our living expenses after local taxes. That way we should appear all above board, what do you reckon to that then?"

The thought of everything they owned from now on being made of gold only warranted one answer, a resounding "Yes" from Harry, Yannie and Dick.

Timorous was immediately sworn to secrecy, but that was not strictly necessary in the circumstances because he knew if Julius or Nero found out, it was a rapid visit by Lastrighticus or a trip to the arena as a light meal for the resident lions.

It took the rest of the group all day to visit the other branches that were being inundated with requests from wealthy Romans and Greeks for the new credit card facility. Yannie imagined he would soon be able to give up taxi driving back home or was it now chariot driving within the next few months.

It was now almost dark as the quartet set off back towards Athinai and not having eaten all day they were looking forward to a meal at their lodgings.

Some hours later they arrived outside Diana's boarding house where they found Hymie Greenberg waiting for them, and his first words were,

"On my life, do you know I have been waiting here all day with your new clothes, so may I try them on you before you eat. Then I can carry out any alterations you may require and then if all is well, present my bill to Nero."

Reluctantly the dusty group agreed providing he acted quickly as they all fancied a bath before eating. Then out of the shadows appeared Ophelia saying, "I have ordered your bath to be ready within the half hour, and your food upon the hour as I am at this moment assisting Diana who managed to sprain her back entertaining clients this very afternoon."

"Come on in then, hurry up," said Tom beckoning to the tailor as they made their way inside the hostel towards the bathing area. Once there they stripped off their dusty clothes and let Hymie try each of their uniforms on them in turn. Luckily for them they all fitted quite admirably, and he left with just the decorations to add to his tailoring.

Yannie was as pleased as punch because each uniform had a built in under garment and he could at last sit in a chariot from then on without damaging his private parts anymore.

When they arrived in the actual bathing area, they were surprised to see that the water was all milky white.

"I'm not getting in that lot," cried Dick.

"Don't be silly now young man it is a special treat for all you men. It is real goats' milk and it is especially for you men for all the help and financial rewards you have brought Diana, Nymphus Cretia, and myself," cried Ophelia appearing from behind the ornate drapes, and eying up the lads equipment.

The dusty group jumped into the milky water, which was warm, and silky to their touch. Ophelia clapped her hands and immediately four young nymphs appeared holding sponges and oils and began cleansing the tired men. Ophelia watched with a glint in her eye as one by one the men began to lose control and became erect as the young girls fingers danced around their naked, milk covered bodies.

Seeing the effects of the young girls' attentions on her men companions Ophelia immediate disrobed herself and leapt into the white milk and dived down looking, or really feeling, for Tom appendage. Before he knew it he was inside of her, not for long however, and as he slipped from her embrace, Dick took his place in more ways than one. Moments later Harry entered her heavenly spot too, whilst Yannie danced around like a demented cow trying to seduce one of the girls. Little did he know they had been forbidden to participate or suffer the wrath of Nymphus Cretia, who being a goddess could wreak all kinds of spells upon them.

Eventually Yannie got his chance with his favourite lady, and was so energetic Tom thought the milk would thicken and begin to turn to cream! Moreover Yannie had his own ideas on cream making as Ophelia could vouch for.

Later after they had all been dried by the young

nymphs, they headed into the eating area, to find their favourite fare of roast duck, chicken, goat and lamb awaiting them, plus copious amounts of wine. Diana was reclining close by on her stomach while a physician massaged her strained back, but as they ate their food and they partook of the wine, it somehow appeared to them that the physician seemed to be massaging more than her back. Yannie thought to himself if I ever strain my back, he can do that to me as well, that's for sure.

The next day Julius arrived quite early and informed them that Nero wished to see them for their inauguration into his court as centurions, and at the same time asked if they had any other schemes in mind that he might profit from.

During the day, which the group of men used as rest time, they began discussing other schemes that they could present to Nero. Suddenly Yannie leaped up into the air and shouted, "I have a brilliant idea," and excitedly explained it to the others.

"What about a Roman taxi service then? I already know all the snags don't I? You three could help design a chariot to hold maybe six or eight people and I reckon if we could put a top on it should go down a treat, what do you reckon then?"

His three former passengers were delighted with his suggestion, so much so that they began to sketch up ideas to present to Nero at their meeting later in the day, and then spent the rest of day discussing various thoughts of their own.

Later in the afternoon Julius called and escorted them to Nero's palace, where after he had enrolled them as centurions and at the same time presented them with a small sword each, he asked if they had any new ideas.

Dick had been selected to present Yannie's taxi chariot idea because being a sales person back home knew the best way to present the scheme.

After listening intently to all the details Nero accepted the need for such a scheme, and gave them the go ahead to organise the manufacture and implementation of the scheme with Julius's help. First they had to arrange the manufacture of a prototype chariot, to be presented to him for approval within the month.

They left the palace with their new swords swinging at their sides; Tom was glad he had on undergarments otherwise he could have suffered an injury from the swinging blade. Then during the following days Julius made a nuisance of himself pestering them for drawings he could present to the local manufacturer. By that time they decided on two types of chariot, one a six seat version and the other with eight seats both to be drawn by two horses. After a final meeting it took two scribes another two days to finish their scale drawings, which Julius, along with Tom this time, took to the local chariot maker. He, a master craftsman, on examining the drawings was quite impressed, and wishing he had thought of the idea himself.

They left his workshop with instructions that Nero required the prototype within the month of August, however he and Tom would visit the workshop regularly and chart his progress. Yannie would also visit the manufacturers daily and check on the quality of the work with him being somewhat of an expert in the field of taxis back home.

A week or two later due to a few problems with the manufacture he had to report to Julius that the project was behind the schedule set by Nero but that the end result should please him. In the meantime would he ask the ruler if either of the two names he was about to suggest would be suitable names for the new service.

Yannie then put to him the two names that were proffered either: Chariotax, or Chaxis Ltd. Julius thought that either might be acceptable and he would put the names forward only when the prototype was ready for its trials and if accepted a company could then be officially formed.

Meanwhile, Tom and his two pals were planning another money making scheme for themselves and also Nero. Tom's first suggestion was that the new company would pay a percentage of its profits to the shareholders whom he suggested should be, Yannie, themselves and Julius, with Nero as Chairman. They thought he would like that position. They also decided that Nero should institute a licensing scheme for the chariot owners to apply for and most importantly of all for the local senate to introduce a Road tax; a proportion of the revenue raised to be used to repair broken bridges and paths etc. From this new licensing fee they should receive five percent per annum as a royalty for thinking up the scheme in the first place, provided Nero agreed. In addition Yannie who thought up the idea should receive a further bonus ex gratis.

Later that month Tom Dick and Harry accompanied Yannie to the manufacturers to view the finished prototype. They were quite impressed with what they saw and Yannie had the inside of his creation adorned with all black leather which they understood this was a throw back to his taxi days back home. The new vehicle also sported a removable canvas top in the event of inclement weather or extremely hot sunshine – the latter being the most likely. Along each side there were oak rubbing strips indented with brass studs and at the front was a protective screen of brass behind which the driver would stand. In front of that was a curved ornamental hammered copper screen to protect the driver from any stones thrown up by the two horses that would be employed to propel it.

The three friends congratulated Yannie on his eye for detail and the quality of the whole unit, however the manufacturer was a little apprehensive at being a few days late with delivery. Tom reassured him that they would inform Nero that the delay was caused only by the sheer craftsmanship involved and it was better to be late and great, than early and unacceptable.

On their return to their lodgings they despatched a runner to inform Julius that the new design could be presented for Nero's inspection the very next day, and he, in turn, sent a return runner to agree the time of presentation that would be at 11am the following morning.

That evening the boys had a good time in the company of their landlady as her torso seemed back to its normal acrobatic self, she had learnt much from Yannie, who had shown her the position he had read about in the Karma Sutra, although he almost cricked his back trying sex on one leg.

His three mates nearly collapsed laughing at his predicament until they saw Diana pick him up and thrust him in her favourite spot as if he was a baby. It was a good job he was only fife feet five thought Tom, if a little enviously.

The night was soon over and the next morning after breakfast the group set off to the manufacturers to collect the prototype taxi. For once they decided to hire an experienced driver to take them to Nero's palace because they just couldn't afford any accidents to their new project.

Just before 11 o'clock they arrived at the palace in a cloud of dust and Yannie remarked, "Who the bloody hell does this driver think he is, Stirling Moss?"

Nobody answered as a crowd of centurions surrounded the vehicle and began pointing at it with admiring glances. Suddenly Nero clapped his hands and Julius bellowed out, "Quiet everyone, and stand back and make way for one Nero II our revered leader."

Everyone stood motionless as Nero approached the new

vehicle, and as the horses were held steady climbed aboard to inspect the taxi in detail. After what seemed like an age he turned to Yannie and remarked, "Well done new centurion and friends, I accept this vehicle and hereby authorise the manufacture of twenty more such creations. I shall name this new service 'Chariotax', that is my proffered name and this will be my decreed law from this moment forth."

He then turned to Julius and pointing to the driver said, "Have that dust creating dog there thrown to the lions this very day." Then he stormed off.

"Ruddy hell that's bit harsh isn't it mates," cried Dick.

Julius pulled him over and whispered in his ear, "It's all right stranger do not worry, he can drive you back and then inform him to go hide in the hills somewhere, because if I ever see him here again he will definitely be lion meat." Then he too turned and followed Nero into the palace.

The driver who had in the meanwhile collapsed, was hastily revived by Yannie, who gave him a swift kick up the bottom, and muttered, "Quick, Stirling take us to the manufacturers again, pronto." Although the driver did not understand the word 'pronto' he immediately got the message as the group climbed aboard and they disappeared in another cloud of dust.

When they arrived at the manufacturer's workshop he was standing outside ringing his hands. On seeing them he rushed over and asked, "Are things alright and did Nero approve especially as we were late, I was imagining a visit from Lastrighticus, instead of you lot?"

"Everything is fine Marcus, he was extremely pleased and we are authorised to place an order with you for another twenty units. Each one is to be sign-written on either side and at the rear with the name Chariotax Service in gold and silver lettering. There is also one other addition, each unit will require a secure box positioned at the drivers side, for him to accept payment in cash only, none of the new type credit cards will be acceptable." Tom's new that it would then be easier to cream off some of the cash before it was deposited for safe keeping in one of the new banks.

The manufacturer knelt down and kissed his hand saying, "Thank you stranger you have saved my life and my business, how can I reward you?"

"Shut up Yannie, later mate, later just be patient, alright," he said glaring at his Greek friend who was about to butt in on the conversation.

Standing upright the manufacturer asked the group of friends, "Where is that silly driver over there running to, we haven't even paid him yet?"

"I think he has been taken short, it's all the dust you know," volunteered Yannie.

Then the group after a celebration drink with Marcus the chariot manufacturer, left in another hired chariot for their lodgings for another meal and a bath before retiring for the night.

Moving to the end of the month we find Yannie doing his quality control check on the completed vehicles, while Tom, Dick and Harry had been setting up a central base for the Chariotax chariots to operate from, and Julius and his scribes were drawing up the necessary permits to be countersigned by Nero.

He had also been inundated with applications for the permits and had made quite a few Denarii on the side for the privilege of granting them. He found he now had enough silver coins to melt down and have an ornamental goblet made and felt he could not then be caught fiddling.

Tom had suggested to him earlier a tariff of charges and it was agreed that the following would stand as fares. However Julius, Tom, Dick, Harry and Yannie would carry a free pass allowing them to ride without paying.

The charges were set as follows:

1 mile	One Quadrans
2-4 miles	Two Quadrantes
5-10 miles	Two Semis
10-20.1.1	Two Dupondius
Over 20	Two Sesterlus or One Aureus

This tariff was to be displayed inside each vehicle behind the driver, Yannie suggested a further idea that he hoped would make him some extra cash, and after discussing his idea with the others and Julius it was agreed he would give each potential driver, in effect a driving test. Of course a small fee, of two gold Aureus per lesson was agreed.

Yannie reckoned if he personally were not ever to return to London, at least he would be one of the richest business operators in Greece.

The taxi service began in September of that year 52, and soon proved a great success. So much so that a further twenty new chariots for taxi use were commissioned by Julius and Nero, much to the delight of Marcus the manufacturer.

The chariots in the meantime had also been upgraded with design changes after the initial trial period that indicated a lack of comfort on the longer journeys. These included extra padding to the seats the addition of grab handles and the fitting of a form of springing to the undercarriage of the vehicle.

Yannie was rubbing his hands in glee because these modifications increased the price of each chariot significantly and his share of that cost also increased.

The rest of the group's enterprises, the spas and the banks were also now raking in a mountain of money for them all so they decided they might as well build a Villa for themselves close to one of the banks. They also wanted to help their landlady Diana completely refurbish her boarding house in the meantime, as they waited anxiously whilst their new Villa plans were approved by Nero II.

Julius informed them he could hurry up the application for a small gratuity. The lads however decided to turn him down saying that they were still saving very hard for the materials, because they dare not let on that they were making extra money on the side, – in fact a great deal of it, to be precise.

The next few weeks saw them working hard with some local decorators and builders converting Diana's and their present digs into what looked more like a first class hotel. Tom suggested she should now reduce their rent, and increase everyone else's that decided to stay there. She was over the moon at the suggestion, then thanks to some crafty advertising placed by Yannie in the inside of the new taxi fleet, her business began to flourish to such an extent she had to recruit four extra deposed young goddesses to satisfy her customers carnal needs. She did however, reserve her own favours just for the three rugby players and especially Yannie. In the refurbishment they had added a sound proofed room that held many strange objects of torture, but none of the boys fancied trying out her special services especially in that particular area, with the thought of pain with no gain!

When all the conversion work was completed she decided to throw another party to celebrate, and invited Julius Marcus the manufacturer and Sinus Timorous because she thought he would be the one person for her to carry out a test of the new sound proofing as she knew he liked to be dominated.

When Julius arrived and saw the new decorations that were quite different to those usually seen in Greece, he was most exited and informed Tom he would mention the fact to Nero who might commission them to modify his own private love nest.

He seemed really impressed by all the privacy afforded to whosoever used that particular facility and that, he thought, should go down well with his master Nero who at times sought privacy from his court of officials and hangers on.

Diana decided that on the party night she would invite some other gods and centurions to take part later that night in a special orgy session. She invited All Alonis, the lonely lover, Sinus Conquerus another legendary lover, one Marco Gigolo a womanising god, Aqua Erectus a horny master slave, and last but no means least Unctuous Uranus the queer royal guard who sported the largest appendage in the land. Then just in case she could not cope with all of the men she also invited Ophelia Letushavit and Nymphus Cretia her over sexed female friends.

When the group of friends saw the guest list they felt like taking a holiday in one of their own spas, however it wasn't quite the right time of the year so they got together and vowed to protect each other from the likes of Unctuous and Aqua Erectus. Yannie decided he would have a cod piece with a bottom cover plate made of bronze that very day as he didn't fancy unwittingly bending over in the presence of Unctuous, just in case the Royal guard was slightly drunk and ready, willing and able.

Tom suggested jokingly that Yannie could always stick his sword up his tunic to stop himself bending over Yannie's reply that day was quite unprintable.

The night of the party arrived and the guests flocked inside and were ushered into the newly constructed dining area where they found an abundance of food and copious amounts of drink just for their consumption. However quite soon the building rocked to roars of laughter as a troop of less than manly young men cavorted around a raised stage doing an impression of a girls' harem. Julius, sitting next to Unctuous, slid his sword under the guard's toga and indicated he was to stay put, well at least for the time being. "Later perhaps" he whispered, eyeing the huge bulge in his white toga.

The three ladies of the house were beginning to unwind as they drank wine from silver goblets while cavorting about completely naked and avoiding with the utmost of skills the attempts by nearly all and sundry to grab them and seduce them.

While they danced around they repeatedly cried, "Later men later, we have all night yet!"

Yannie, sitting in a corner, thought he would be lucky if he lasted until midnight as he was so inflamed by Ophelia's dancing. It took Tom and Dick with a form of rugby hold to contain him on his seat.

Some time later just after midnight, Tom noticed Nymphus leading Sinus Timorous up the steps towards the newly constructed 'chamber of horrors' as he had nicknamed it.

Yannie also spotted her actions and whispered to the others, and forgetting his lust for Ophelia, "How about us four taking a look at what's going on in the old special room then? I forgot to let you know she and I have had some viewing tubes made, and we intend to charge the Roman visitors or any lodgers two Sesterlus a time to view the action going on inside. And do you see those two huge eunuchs standing at the top of the stairway over there? They count the time viewed with a water clock then close the tube off unless the viewing person pays a couple more pieces of silver. Great don't you think?"

"Trust you to think up something like that you little Greek arsehole. You're not in Soho now you know, anyway I think it's a great idea, don't you Dick?"

However Dick was just sitting there slightly inebriated with his eyes bulging at the news.

"Bloody hell, Yannie who do you think you are, the porn king of London?"

"Well do you realise we lot get to view the action free?" replied his original taxi driver.

"That's different then, shall we go up now?" whispered Harry.

"Two at a time only," whispered the voice of Julius who had been standing behind them ear wigging their conversation, "I want a free pass too or else you little Greek wizard," he added.

"Granted Julius, granted," cried Yannie wishing he had waited a while before informing the others. The group of friends headed up the stairway trying to appear casual as they climbed each step in anticipation. When they arrived outside the oval shaped room they could just discern the whimpering cries of someone in pain and the occasional swish of a whip being wielded. Then they spied in the walls set about two feet apart, what appeared to be a leather covered tube about an inch in diameter.

Pointing at them Yannie remarked, "That's the viewing tubes ten in all, so lets get viewing shall we?"

The group eagerly placed one eye each against a viewing tube, only to stand back and curse because all they saw was total darkness. Julius grabbed Yannie by his left ear placed his sword under his throat and cried, "What my little Greek friend has gone wrong now?"

"I forgot, I haven't told Ophelia to remove the covers from the inside of the tubes yet, because I didn't know she was going to use the room tonight," he stuttered.

Tom thought Julius was going to cut Yannie's throat right there and then, when he suddenly started to laugh out loud. Pointing at one of the eunuchs he shouted, "Look he's got his nose stuck in the tube over there, shall I cut it off for him?"

"By all that is holy Julius, let him and my friend be. I shall discuss with our landlady and her friend Ophelia that a new larger tube to be inserted in the wall expressly for your own viewing pleasure. It will be set on the other side so that you can always view in complete privacy."

Julius lowered his sword as Yannie gulped with relief, and placed it back inside its scabbard. Grabbing Tom's right arm in a Roman clasp, he cried, "Agreed my worthy friend but do keep this dunderhead from the court for two weeks."

Tom knew he had to agree as Yannie muttered to himself, 'mad bastards these Romans' Dick was quietly giggling to himself because Yannie appeared to have lost his suntan and was as white as his freshly washed toga.

The group decided to head back down the stairway to the receding sounds of whimpers of 'mercy mistress, mercy' coming through the massive oak door of the oval room.

When they arrived on the ground floor they were just in time to see Unctuous Uranus enter the rear end of a young man painted all over with gold. This prompted Julius to remark, "One of these days, my sword will depose him of that large obnoxious thing between his legs, then I shall have it pickled and displayed in a jar for future generations to scorn or admire. Come let us drink some more my comrades." Julius guided them towards a large barrel of red wine that was still unopened.

The group of friends spent until the early hours drinking and discussing future plans. Julius told them he could recommend a good Roman architect and builder for their new villa who had been responsible for building Nero's own palace.

Little did they know that Julius also owned a local marble factory, and would therefore make money out of them. Despite them refusing his previous offer of help to speed up their application to build their villa from Nero's planning officials, they did agree to that particular request and toasted their decision with ample amounts of wine, before retiring for the night.

Chapter 10

The Way Back Home

It was now some two months on and getting slightly cooler as the year approached December time. In the meantime the lads had accumulated very large amounts of money and most of it was secreted safely out of the way.

They had recently received the go ahead to build their proposed Villa, and were due to meet the architect that week to discuss their individual preferences. Ophelia suggested she accompany them, and her obvious charms might then help them secure a good deal regarding the building costs. That offer from her was because of their kindness in refurbishing her best friend's boarding house.

Yannie thought that was a great idea, and suggested she wear her see through dress, and paint her nipples red to enhance their size and beauty. Tom agreed but he also suggested Yannie ought to visit a physician about his obsession with large knockers.

Ophelia just laughed and shook her body so that those two large items danced around like potatoes in a sack. Dick had to restrain Yannie otherwise an exhibition of attempted rape would more than likely have taken place.

That weekend they had their first meeting with the architect, and a provisional price and design was agreed, thanks to Ophelia flaunting her undoubted attributes at every occasion she could. The lads were so pleased with her help they suggested they have a private party at her place and they would cover all expenses. Ophelia, never one to turn down a party, immediately agreed and suggested she invite her two other friends Diana and Nymphus Cretia to liven things up a bit as was their want.

The lads of course readily agreed and then after their meeting broke up, they visited a local store to order the wine and ingredients for their party. Whilst they were choosing the items the owner offered to supply them with a new type of aphrodisiac made from sheep's testes.

Yannie didn't care what it was made from as long as it worked. The shopkeeper guaranteed its results and informed them if it didn't work he would refund their monies. Then from behind his hand whispered, "Nero has been using it for months now, but do not divulge this information to anyone or as you now know, one Lastrighticus will be visiting all of us!"

The lads left with their Chariotax filled to overflowing as they headed for Ophelia's abode, while she sat in the back of the taxi with Yannie's hand up her short, diaphanous skirt whilst sporting a big smile on her beautiful countenance.

Later that day after unloading all the goods for the party, Ophelia sent a runner to inform her two friends about the party that evening. In the meantime the boys decided to bathe and prepare themselves for a party that could resemble a hard fought rugby cup match.

When the evening arrived the three women appeared dressed in what can only be described as the flimsiest of outfits and wearing nothing whatsoever underneath. The first thing the boys did was take a large dose of the sheep's parts with their first drink, and then tucked into a gigantic meal that three young nymphs served to them from silver platters.

Much later that evening the boys were now full up with food and a great degree of wine because at least a gallon or two of wine had been consumed between them.

By this time the three women were completely naked and crushing grapes into the ever-willing open mouths of our rugby players, and whispering to each one in turn, "shall we not retire to the bedroom men?"

When suddenly outside, they heard Divinia Mindout the soothsayer calling out "Beware". As her voice faded on the evening breeze, Ophelia stopped her canoodling with Yannie, and said, "Stop a moment my friends, I must find out what she doth say, and give her a small coin to comfort her," and she walked towards the door oblivious of her own nakedness.

She returned moments later, the colour drained from her face as she approached her guests and in a startled voice cried out, "You must depart immediately my friends. Now at this very moment. Divinia has informed me that Nero has discovered that you have been appropriating monies without his knowledge, and you will all be rounded up on the morrow and passed over to Lastrighticus without trial.

Luckily for you all I have already prepared some many months ago an escape plan for you my most trusted of friends. Outside in my stables there is a new Chariotax I received for favours granted to Marcus. It has two of the fastest horses in Greece bridled to it. The Eunuch driver has been instructed to take you to the port of Platia where you will find a boat waiting that will take you to the island of Crete, where you should be safe until this incident is forgotten by Nero. Please hurry my friends before morning arrives."

The three rugby mates and Yannie looked at each other in amazement, and the first to speak was Tom.

"That's torn it we'll never get home now. Anyway I'm not leaving without my hoard of silver, so lets all load up shall we?" he said turning to the other three.

Ophelia interrupted him by saying, "Let my eunuchs

do that for you, while we all have a farewell session upstairs, that should take your minds off your troubles for a while."

The boys, in spite of their fears, immediately agreed. They might not get another good shagging ever again, so they accompanied the girls upstairs wildly stripping off their clothes as they went!

That last night of sex was the best they had ever experienced especially with the help of the crushed sheep's bits. However around two a.m. they very reluctantly left their female companions and, grabbing their old twenty-first century clothing just in case Crete had a colder climate, they kissed the women goodbye and climbed into the Chariotax. Tom prodded the driver and they were off into the darkness in a cloud of dust. Ophelia shouted, "I instructed the driver to take the short way over the mountains." Her last farewell faded into the night air as the Chariotax gathered speed.

An hour later after a long uphill climb their taxi reached the peak of the mountain as the driver cracked his whip and the vehicle gathered speed heading down towards the port of Platia.

The friends were now being bounced around like rodeo riders as the taxi went ever faster downhill much to Yannie's consternation. He screamed at the driver, "Slow down you African ponce you."

"Don't be bloody silly Yannie he can't understand a word!"

"Give the silly bastard a whack then," shouted Dick still hanging on for grim death.

Suddenly they came upon a bend and the driver could not stop the vehicle as brakes had not been invented yet, and to screams of anguish from all the occupants the whole vehicle, silver treasure and all, headed straight over the cliff edge towards oblivion.

Meanwhile back in the twenty-first century a lone police constable was approaching an empty taxi, parked with one wheel on the kerb and with its meter still running.

Speaking into his walkie-talkie radio he remarked to control, "Guess what I've found down here Sarge some bloody fools parked a taxicab on the pavement with its engine still running so can you meet me just off Greenwich High Street? I reckon this one will be a good pinch?"

By that time he had actually reached the parked driverless taxi, and was nosing at the empty back seat trying to fathom out what had happened, when into view strolled his overweight Sergeant pulling out his own notebook.

The constable was now leaning inside the offside looking at the meter with ten pounds sixty pence registered on the dial, and as he turned to greet his sergeant he inadvertently moved the meter lever back to zero.

Immediately inside the taxi three rugby players found themselves trying to get up in the rear of the taxi, as Yannie, now sitting in the driving seat leaned back and shouted, "Sorry you fellows some silly cow stepped out in front of me, so when you get up don't touch that red lever all right?"

The Sergeant had now arrived and was staring at the three occupants dressed in tee shirts and jeans. Hearing Yannie's outburst he pulled the young constable aside and in a menacing whisper asked him, "You been drinking lad, or are you on something else? Because as you can see you silly sod there are three blokes in the back and a driver's still in it so how do you explain your call in then?"

The constable looked inside the taxi, and almost fainted as he said, "Sorry Sarge must have got the sun in my eyes, I could swear it was empty though."

He was interrupted, by Yannie asking, "Can we go

now these blokes are late for the theatre as it is, and you want to prosecute that old cow over there for jay walking. Bloody menace these old people."

"Get on your way son, and remember you will be old one day," said the sergeant sarcastically.

Yannie drove on towards the Coliseum where he left the three friends and headed off to have his paid for meal.

When the three mates had purchased their tickets, a troupe of buskers nearby caught their eye, who were made up of three girls doing acrobatics all were very flimsily dressed.

Tom looked at his two mates and said, "Do those three birds over there remind you two of anyone?"

"Can't say they do, but I think we both have a feeling we have seen them before somewhere, but where don't ask us," they both replied in unison.

Yannie in the meantime was sitting in a café eating a Kebab trying to understand why his meter only registered three quid thus far and thought, I must get that fixed on Monday.

The End.